The Cranky Day

and Other Thomas the Tank Engine Stories

Random House 🏠 New York

A Random House Pictureback® Book

Photographs by David Mitton for Britt Allcroft's production of Thomas the Tank Engine and Friends.

Britt Allcroft's Thomas & Friends based on The Railway Series by The Rev W Awdry.
Copyright © Britt Allcroft (Thomas) LLC 2000. Photographs © Britt Allcroft (Thomas) Ltd 1998. All rights reserved.
THOMAS & FRIENDS is a trademark of Britt Allcroft Inc in the USA, Mexico, and Canada and of Britt Allcroft (Thomas) Limited in the rest of the world. THE BRITT ALLCROFT COMPANY is a trademark of The Britt Allcroft Company plc. Published in the United States of America by Random House, Inc., New York
and simultaneously in Canada by Random House of Canada Limited, Toronto.
www.randomhouse.com/kids
www.thomasthetankengine.com
Library of Congress Cataloging-in-Publication Data:
Thomas the tank engine: Cranky bugs and other Thomas stories / photographs by David Mitton for Britt Allcroft's production of Thomas the tank engine and friends. p. cm. — (Random House pictureback book)
"Based on The railway series by the Rev. W. Awdry." Contents: Cranky bugs—Put-upon Percy—Lady Hatt's birthday party.
ISBN 0-375-80246-0
[1. Railroads—Trains—Fiction.] I. Mitton, David, ill. II. Awdry, W. Railway series. III. Thomas the tank engine and friends.
PZ7.T36957 2000 [E]—dc21 99-35492
Printed in the United States of America   April 2000   10 9 8 7 6 5 4 3 2 1
PICTUREBACK, RANDOM HOUSE and colophon, and PLEASE READ TO ME and colophon are registered trademarks of Random House, Inc.

CRANKY BUGS

Thomas and Percy enjoyed working in the docks. They liked the sea air and the sound of the gulls. But one day, the friends were feeling hot and bothered. A crane was causing trouble. His name was Cranky, and this was his first day at the docks.

"You're useless little bugs," he called from above. "If you put these freight cars on the inside lines, then I wouldn't have so far to travel."

"Rubbish!" said Thomas. "No crane has ever complained before."

"Well, I'm complaining now." And Cranky banged his load down on the quayside.

Later, the two engines met Gordon and James and told them about Cranky.

"Cranes are airy-fairy things. They need a lot of attention—like me, in fact," said Gordon. "You should see the situation from Cranky's point of view. He's high up in the air, coping with wind, rain, and baking sun, then he looks down and sees you two little engines being annoying. No wonder he calls you bugs."

When Cranky heard that the big engines agreed with him, he grew bossier still.

"Come on, come on—push those freight cars closer to me." But Percy was too upset to concentrate and pushed the freight cars too far. Poor Percy!

Then Cranky played a trick on Thomas.

"Push your freight cars onto the outside line. It's easier for me to load up."

So Thomas did. But Cranky left the loads *beside* the freight cars, not in them.

"You must have known my arm can't reach you there," complained Cranky.

This mix-up caused confusion and delay. Sir Topham Hatt was most upset.

"Thomas and Percy, this new crane has an important job to do. I have heard that you have not been helping him today. You will go to your sheds and consider how you will improve yourselves tomorrow."

Now Thomas and Percy were upset, too.

That evening, a big storm raged across the island. Cranky and the engines were trapped at the docks.

"We're sure to be safe in this shed," said Duck.

But he was wrong. The engines had no idea that they were about to be put in great danger by an old tramp steamer. It was out of control and running around, straight into the sheds.

"A-a-agh!"

"Heeeeelp!" called the engines from inside the shed.

"I can't," called Cranky.

When the storm was over, Sir Topham Hatt rushed to the scene of destruction.

"Thomas and Percy will help you," he called to Cranky. "And then you can help the engines."

"Oh, please hurry," cried Cranky. "And tell them I'm sorry I was rude to them."

"So it was you," murmured Sir Topham Hatt. "I owe those engines an apology."

Thomas and Percy soon came to the rescue.

And it wasn't too long before Cranky was upright again and clearing the wreckage. At last, all the engines were free.

"Oh, thank you," said Gordon. "What would I have done without you?"

"Well, I had to be rescued before I could help you. But I never thought it would be by a couple of b-b—" Cranky was about to say "bugs," but he quickly corrected himself. "Er…small engines. Thank you. I'll never be rude again. However, you two mites are in my way, so move over."

"Pah!" said Percy. "He's back to bugging us!"

"Don't move! You're still attached to Cranky!"

But it was too late.

Cranky still looks down on the two little engines, but ever since that stormy night, he never calls them "bugs" or "mites," because he knows they may bite back.

PUT-UPON PERCY

Percy puffed grumpily into the yards. He was feeling put-upon and said so.

"I feel put-upon," he complained to Thomas.

Thomas was confused. "Put upon what? The rails?"

"No. Put-upon with work. Driver says *he* is, too."

"Put-upon. What a silly saying!" replied Thomas.

But Annie and Clarabel liked it, and they sang about it, too.

"Percy's been put upon,
Put upon,
Put upon.
Percy's been put upon.
Poor old Percy!"

"Percy *is* being put upon.
I am! I am! I am!"

He collected metal from the foundry, coal from the yards, flour from the mills, rock from the quarries, and fuel from the depot. Then he delivered it all to the docks. Next, he collected some empty freight cars.

"Who's this dirty little engine?" cried the freight cars. "We want Thomas or Duck!"

Percy ignored them.

"Put-upon, put-upon, that's what I am."

That night, all the engines laughed at him.

"We can see what's been put upon you!" said Thomas.

"Silence," said Sir Topham Hatt. "Percy, you've done a good day's work. Now get a good night's rest."

"Yes, sir. Thank you, sir."

Next morning, he took some freight cars to the coal yards. Then he had to push empty freight cars to the mine shaft.

When he arrived, there was trouble. The foreman spoke to his driver.

"The freight cars are stuck on the mechanism. All they need is a good push."

"We'll do it right away."

Percy shunted back to where a large canvas barrier was used to protect his line from loose rocks. Percy charged at the line of freight cars—too fast and too hard.

"Oh, no!" gasped Percy. The freight cars broke free but ran out of control to the mines below.

"On, on, faster, faster!" the silly freight cars yelled. Then there was trouble again.

"Get out of here fast! The mine's collapsing!"

"We'll just have to make a run for it, Percy!" called his driver.

"There's going to be an avalanche!" wailed Percy. And he was right. Worse still, the track he was on began to crumble.

"Oh, help!" wailed Percy. Then he remembered something he had seen earlier.

"There's a canvas barrier by the track—that might save us!"

They were just in time.

Percy was right. The canvas did indeed save them. But the miners didn't know that.

"The avalanche has buried an engine and its crew!" shouted the foreman. "We must help them."

When Percy had been rescued, Sir Topham Hatt spoke to his driver and fireman, then to Percy.

"Driver told me how brave you were, Percy. As a reward, you will be repainted at the works!"

"Oh, thank you, sir!"

When he returned, Percy's coat glistened in the sun.

"I'm sorry we teased you, Percy," said Thomas. "You were certainly put upon by that avalanche."

"Yes, indeed, but just look at my new coat of paint. Now, I don't mind *that* being put upon me."

LADY HATT'S BIRTHDAY PARTY

One summer's day, Thomas and Percy were idling in the station when Bertie the bus arrived.

"Have you noticed something?" said Bertie.

"What sort of something?" asked Thomas.

"Sir Topham Hatt. He seems, well, different," replied Bertie.

"I did see him staring at the clouds this morning," said Percy. "I wonder why."

The reason was simple. It was Lady Hatt's birthday, and Sir Topham had a new outfit.

"It's perfect for my birthday party," said his wife. "You'll look splendid, Topham dear."

"And I'll wear my finest hat just for you," he replied. "Your birthday is a great occasion."

"It is. So don't be late."

"Don't worry, my dear. I shall be spick-and-span and right on time!"

Later that day, Sir Topham Hatt had changed into his new suit.

"You look fine, sir," said the stationmaster. "You'd best be going."

"Indeed," agreed Sir Topham Hatt. "The engines are busy—I'll take the car."

"Is it reliable?" asked the stationmaster.

"Certainly," said Sir Topham Hatt.

But it wasn't. As he sped along, he suddenly saw a large hole in the road. He braked hard, but it was too late.

"Bother! Now I've got a puncture. If I change my wheel, I am sure to dirty my suit, and that would never do."

Just then, he heard Caroline. "I have to attend my wife's birthday party and I cannot be late. Please give me a lift."

"I'll try, sir." But Caroline didn't like going fast. "I'm hot. My engine will overheat." And it did. "Told you so," said Caroline sadly.

"Bother, bother."

Then he heard a loud whistle. It was George the steamroller. George was cross when he saw Caroline.

"Call yourself a car? You're a disgrace to the road. Find yourself a scrapyard." Caroline spluttered in fury.

George's driver was more polite.

"Can I be of assistance, sir?"

"Only if you can get me to my wife's birthday party," sighed Sir Topham Hatt.

"We can take you to Thomas," replied the driver. "He's just down the line."

"Much obliged." And they rumbled away.

"What about me?" wailed Caroline.

"I'll send for help," called Sir Topham Hatt. "Stay there."

"That's all I *can* do."

George was enjoying rolling along the lane, but not Sir Topham Hatt. Oil splashed everywhere. Worse was to follow.

"Help!" cried George. "Something's snapped!"
He veered out of control, and Sir Topham Hatt landed in a muddy ditch close to where Thomas was taking on water.

"Bother, bother!"
Thomas had never seen Sir Topham Hatt in such a mess.

"Can I help you, sir?" asked Thomas' driver.

"Yes, please. Get me to the station as fast as you can."

"I'm afraid our fireman's been taken ill."

"Then I'll be your fireman," sighed Sir Topham Hatt.

Thomas was excited.

Sir Topham Hatt had to work hard. Coal dust and smut flew everywhere.

At last they reached the station. Sir Topham Hatt looked at the clock. "Just in time," he gasped. He hurriedly picked up a huge bunch of flowers.
"Good luck!" called Thomas.

Sir Topham Hatt's wife was waiting for him.

As the clock struck three, there stood Sir Topham Hatt, tired but triumphant. He gave his wife the flowers.

"Well, thank you, my dear. I knew this was my special birthday party, but I didn't know it was fancy dress!"

Everyone laughed, and then the party began.